The Lazy Bed

Dr Anshumali Pandey

 pencil

ISBN 978-93-5458-264-6
© Dr Anshumali Pandey 2021
Published in India 2021 by Pencil

A brand of

One Point Six Technologies Pvt. Ltd.
123, Building J2, Shram Seva Premises,
Wadala Truck Terminal, Wadala (E)
Mumbai 400037, Maharashtra, INDIA
E connect@thepencilapp.com
W www.thepencilapp.com

DISCLAIMER: *This is a work of fiction. Names, characters, places, events and incidents are the products of the author's imagination. The opinions expressed in this book do not seek to reflect the views of the Publisher.*

Author biography

Dr. Anshumali Pandey is a renowned name in the field of Hospitality Tourism and Tribal Food. He is a Chef and a Teacher by profession, and also an author, business auditor, and an avid culinary traveller to the Sub continental hinterlands.

Books written by the Author are -
1. Theory of Indian Cookery,
2. Beauty and Irony of Silvassa Tourism,
3. A Short Indian Food Story,
4. Be Your Own Guide to Indian Cuisine (Paperback & Kindle),
5. Cookery Fundamentals, being an Indian Chef.
6. History of Indian Food (Paperback & Kindle),
7. Personal Budget: Easy Work Book,
8. The Great Indian Story Book for Children (Paperback & Kindle),
09. Dictionary Making Work Book for Children.

Queries are welcomed: anshumali.pandey@gmail.com

CONTENTS

The Lucky Portuguese in India

On 2nd August 1954, the small Portuguese enclave of Dadra and Nagar Haveli in India, sandwiched between Maharashtra and Gujarat (Indian States) was liberated by Indian freedom fighters.

The interesting story is, how Dadra & Nagar Haveli went into Portuguese hands, in the first place?

In the 16th century, the Portuguese were on a roll establishing their stronghold over India. In 1510, they conquered Goa from the Adilshahs of Bijapur. This was followed by quick conquests of the northern part of the west coast of India. The Portuguese acquired Daman (1531); Salsette, Bombay, and Vasai (1534); and Diu in 1535. Within 25 years the Portuguese province stretched from Chaul on the Konkan coast to the island of Diu, which they lorded over for 200 years, until the Maratha's came.

In 1739 the Portuguese faced a near wipe-out. In the Maratha-Portuguese war in 1739, the Marathas under Bajirao's brother Chimaji Appa captured Vasai and with it most of the Portuguese territories apart from the little towns of Daman and Diu.

However, Dadra & Nagar Haveli was never a part of the Portuguese colonies in India to begin with. They actually went to Portuguese as a part of a 'compensation package' and remained with them through an strangeness of fate.

Till the 1780s, the pargana or administrative unit of Dadra & Nagar Haveli were under Maratha rule. Sometime in 1772, Janoji Dhulap, the commander of the Maratha navy had confiscated a Portuguese Warship named 'Santana' and sunk it. The outraged Portuguese had sent an ambassador to the Peshwa's court in Pune demanding compensation.

At this time, the Maratha court was in chaos with several claimants to the throne. Also the first Anglo-Maratha war had ended in 1782 and the Salsette Island had been ceded to the British. The Maratha courtiers didn't want added trouble, with the Portuguese mounting an offensive against them, or worse joining forces with the British.

To counter this in 1783, as a 'friendly gesture' the Maratha court offered the revenue from the 71 villages of Nagar Haveli as 'compensation' for the loss of the ship Santana. This was followed up by adding the revenue of Dadra, to the Portuguese kitty two years later. The deal was that the Portuguese would recover the cost of the sunken ship from the revenue and then return Dadra and Nagar Haveli back to the Marathas.

Fortune however had something else in store. The turmoil and infighting at the Maratha court meant that no one actually asked the Portuguese to return these areas. So busy were they fighting within, that they forgot to claim what belonged to them. The collapse of the Maratha Empire in 1818 after the third Anglo-Maratha war closed this episode and these areas remained with the Portuguese all the way till 1954.

On the night of 22 July 1954, Indian freedom fighters under the leadership of Waman Desai and Francis Mascarenhas sneaked into the territory of Dadra and took over the local police station, which had only three personnel. Soon other volunteers overpowered the Portuguese authorities and started taking over the villages. On 2nd August 1954, Silvassa, the capital was liberated and finally the Portuguese rule in these areas ended.

In the colonial history of India, the story of Dadra and Nagar Haveli, which were literally handed over and forgotten..., is truly only one of its kind.

The Emperor's Daughters

A long time ago, a wealthy Emperor had three beautiful daughters. They had everything they wanted offered to them on a platter of gold. However, only one thing was lacking in their life, none of them had a husband, nor did they have a suitor. This made the Emperor very unhappy. He had food, but he could not eat. What shall we do now?

He asked his wife. I want my children to be happily married, but they think that no one is good enough for them. The Emperor's daughters' were however not bothered. "I want to marry the richest man alive," said the oldest sister. "I want to marry the most handsome man," the younger sister said arrogantly. As for the youngest sister, "I want to marry a Emperor like my father. Only he will be richer and more powerful. Oh! What a life I shall live being the queen of a great empire." Their mother the queen added, "Whoever marries my daughters will be a lucky man, seeing how beautiful they all are. Oh no! My daughters will only marry the best men in the whole land."

The Emperor's heart was very troubled. He told his wife, "I'm finding my daughters men who will love and care for them. I will not watch them grow old without husbands and children." Do whatever you want, said the queen, but my daughters will only marry anyone who can tell their names. That way, I will be sure they are marrying the wisest man in the entire land.

It was announced throughout the land, that the Emperor wanted the wisest man to marry his children. Whoever could tell their names would be given their hands in marriage. The rich and famous went with gifts to the palace to try but they couldn't guess the princesses' names. No one ever called them by their real names. Everyone called them "the princesses".

Soon, every available man in the land had gone to ask for the princesses' hands in marriage, but no one could tell their names. So, the tortoise, a very crafty animal decided he would give it a try. But before he went to the palace, he sneaked around the princesses, following them everywhere without their knowledge. Just when the tortoise started to think there was no hope for him, luck smiled on him one day. The princesses went apple picking on the outskirts of the town. The youngest princess was so excited that she started singing. As she sang, she called her older sister by her real name. The younger sister rushed over, and she did the same, calling their oldest sister. They ended up singing together, dancing and calling each other's name. That was how the tortoise knew all their names.

He went to the palace and told the Emperor. The whole town gathered, and the tortoise said the name of each princess. Everyone was shocked. The Emperor had no choice but to give all his daughters to the tortoise as his wives. The princesses and the queen were extremely sad. But there was nothing anyone could do. And so, the tortoise started to take the princesses home as his wives. On their way to tortoise' home, the princesses were so ashamed, that they each chose a very different lifestyle rather than become the tortoise' wife.

And so it happened that since that day, no one ever saw any of the princesses again. The Emperor and queen were very sad, but there was nothing anyone could do. If only the princesses and their mother had known, they would not have been so proud and arrogant in choosing their husbands.

Test of Swami's

SWAMI VIVEKANAND'S inspiring personality is now well known in India and abroad. But, originally this unknown monk of India suddenly rose to fame at the Parliament of Religions held in Chicago (USA) in 1893, representing Hinduism. His vast knowledge of Eastern and Western culture as well as his deep spiritual insight, brilliant conversational skills, empathy and colourful personality made a mark on the hearts of many. Those who happened to see or hear Swami Vivekanand even once, cherish his memory ever after.

Before leaving for abroad for the first time to preach Hinduism, Vivekanand's mother wanted to know whether he is all perfect for this mission or not, she invited him for dinner. Vivekanand enjoyed the food that had the additional flavour of his mother's special love and affection. After the delicious dinner, Vivekanand's mother offered Vivekanand a dish of fruits and a knife. Vivekanand cut the fruit, ate it and after that his mother said, "Son, can you please give me the knife, I need it." Vivekanand immediately responded by giving the knife.

Vivekanand's mother calmly said, "Son, you have passed my test and I heartily bless you for going abroad." Vivekanand surprisingly asked, "Mother, how did you test me? I didn't understand."

Mother replied, "Son, when I asked for the knife, I saw how you handed it to me, you gave the knife by holding its sharp edge and kept the wooden handle of knife towards me. This way, I would not get hurt when I take it and this means you took care of me. And this was your test in which you passed.
The person who thinks of others welfare rather than thinking about oneself has got the right of preaching the world and you have got that right. You have all my blessings."

This was the most important mark he left in the hearts of many he met in his lifetime - to think of others before thinking for oneself.

Moral: The true noble person is the one who thinks of other's happiness even if it is in little matters to our day to day life. The one who thinks of himself alone is considered selfish & will not be valued by the world in the long run. It is the law of nature that as the bigger hearted & noble you become, the more you will keep receiving & as the narrower minded you become, the less you will receive.

The Ego Escape

It was a hot, sunny day in India. Elephant was walking down the path on his way to his favourite water hole. He was looking forward to the cool water and a mud bath.

A Lion was also walking along the path. The Lion was on his way to the grassy plains. He was going to lie down and wait for his lunch. Elephant turned the corner and lifted his trunk in the air. He smelt the water at the water hole. Lion turned into the same corner. He was getting closer to his favourite hunting spot.
Suddenly the two animals met in the middle of the path. "Out of my way," roared the lion. "Out of my way," trumpeted the elephant. "Make way for the king of the jungle," growled the lion. "Certainly not! Where shall I go?" answered the elephant.

The path was blocked. The two strong animals stood facing each other. The elephant would not move. The lion would not move. Other animals began to walk along the path. Some were standing behind the elephant and others behind the lion.

Lion and elephant just stared at each other and refused to move. A monkey came running past. He greeted the other animals. Then he reached the lion and the elephant. He looked at the fierce lion. He looked at the enormous elephant.

The monkey started to chuckle. He ran o into the jungle to get some 'monkey vine' that hung from the trees. He rushed back to the lion and the elephant. "I know how to solve your problem," said the monkey.

All the animals behind the elephant and the lion wanted to get a look at what was going on. They saw the monkey arrive with a long piece of monkey vine. He tied one end around the elephant and the other around the lion. He stood on an anthill nearby and shouted! "Friends, we are going to have a tug of war. When I say 'heave' then it is time for the lion and the elephant to pull the monkey vine!" "May the best animal win," shouted the monkey.

Elephant was very strong and pulled hard at the rope. Lion dug his extra sharp claws into the path and pulled hard too. Suddenly there was a clap of thunder! The animals looked up into the sky. They saw huge dark rain clouds. A storm was on its way.

Then lion felt the first drops of rain. He let go of the monkey vine and ran into the bushes. "My mane, my beautiful mane. I combed it as smooth as silk this morning!" he cried.

 "I win," cried elephant, as he stood in the rain. Elephant's thick skin was like a raincoat. He was not worried about getting wet.

Monkey hopped about with delight. He wanted elephant to win. Suddenly all the animals heard a mighty roar! "No, rain stopped play, there is no contest."
Lion did not want the animals to think he had lost. No contest meant there was no winner.

Elephant nodded his head and walked down the path. He did not care if he got wet and he was looking forward to getting muddy too.

The Funny Hat

Sunny, the big black cat, lay across the mat fast asleep. He was a very big, fat cat. Sunny looked as if he was asleep, but he really had one eye open all the time. Sunny's one eye was looking right at the hole in the wall where a family of five rats lived. Five little frightened rats were peeping out from behind the hole in the wall. The five rats wanted to get away from the big, black cat.

Sunny yawned and stretched and turned over to sleep a bit longer. The rats were quivering with excitement. Now was their chance to escape. One rat tiptoed out to cross the room. He started to run towards the door. Suddenly the door opened! In walked a tall man wearing a top hat. The man threw the top hat onto a chair but it missed the chair and fell on the floor.

Sunny jumped up and hissed. The rat ran back to his hole with the other rats. The chance to escape had gone. Slowly Sunny went back to sleep. The rats looked at the cat and then they noticed the top hat lying on the floor and it gave them an idea.

The rats nodded to each other as they made a plan. They would hide under the hat and see if they could sneak past the big, black cat. Carefully, one by one, they wriggled under the hat and waited. The rats heard Sunny snoring. They thought they would start to walk towards the door under the shelter of the hat. Slowly the hat slid across the floor. The cat did not wake up.

The rats reached the door. It was open just enough for them to slip out and go on down the road. The hat, with the rats, went out of the door. At the same time Sunny woke up. His greedy eyes saw the hat moving across the steps and out of the door. He jumped up and started to walk towards the door. The rats knew they would have to start to run.

The cat was getting closer and the rats could see no escape. Behind them was the cat and in front of them was the road and it led to a duck pond. Oh, what should they do? Whoosh, a sudden gust of wind blew down the road. It tipped the hat over and the rats fell inside. They hung on tightly. What would happen now?

The hat blew down the road and into the pond. The rats peeped over the edge. They saw that they were floating on the pond. Now the hat was a boat!
Sunny looked at the rats floating on the pond. He was very angry. He could not swim. The rats had escaped in their funny top hat. The little rats laughed at the cat. Sunny hissed and went home.

Twinkle Kitten

Twinkle was a little, grey kitten. She had a white spot on his back and a black spot on his nose. Twinkle lived with his mum and two sisters on a farm. Twinkle's sisters were white with black spots. Both of his sisters were very good. Twinkle was the naughty one. She was always getting into trouble.

Twinkle was very adventurous. She wanted to explore the farm. One day she went out into the farmyard to see what was in the big wide world. Twinkle said to herself, "I am not afraid of anything!"

Suddenly a big monster roared out of the garage and sent Twinkle spinning into the bushes. She did not know what had roared past. She picked himself up and decided it was time to go home. Twinkle looked left and she looked right, but there was nowhere that looked like home. She was lost.

'Oh dear,' Twinkle thought. 'Now what shall I do?' She walked across a field and suddenly she stopped! There in front of her was a furry, white animal with spots on its back. Twinkle thought it must be one of her sisters.

Twinkle ran up to the furry, spotted animal. "Can you take

me home?" asked Twinkle. "No," said the furry animal. "You do not belong in my home". "Look at you, you do not have big ears and you do not hop like me," said the furry animal.

Twinkle realized she did not belong with this animal. Twinkle ran to the farmyard where she saw another spotty animal. It was a bit bigger than Twinkle, but it had spots on its back. Twinkle ran up to the spotty animal. "Can I come home with you? You look just like me with all those spots," said Twinkle.

The big animal grunted and jumped into a mud puddle. "I have mud spots on my back. Come and roll in the mud if you want mud spots," said the muddy spotty animal. "No thanks," said Twinkle. She did not want to get muddy. Twinkle ran away again.

Twinkle was getting worried. She was hungry too. Then Twinkle saw another spotted animal. This animal had a loud voice. "Ru, ru," said the voice. "Can I help you?" Twinkle just nodded. She felt himself being lifted up and carried away. A spotty dog had found Twinkle. She scratched at the front door. A little girl opened the door. She jumped up and down.

She was so happy to see the spotty dog and the kitten. She took Twinkle right back to her mother. She was lying in a basket in the kitchen. Twinkle saw his mum and his two sisters. Twinkle listened to their soft purring. "Purr, purr," said the other kittens. They were happy too.

Twinkle was put back in her basket. She felt happy as she snuggled up with his family. She was safe now and she was going to get some milk for his supper.

Witty Minister

The Sadhu

Akbar came to the throne when he was only thirteen years old. In the years that followed, he built on of the greatest empires of his time. He lived in unimaginable splendor. He was surrounded by courtiers who agreed with every word he said, who flattered him and treated him as if he were a god.

Perhaps it was not surprising that Emperor Akbar was sometimes arrogant and behaved as if the whole world belonged to him. One day, Birbal decided to make the great emperor stop and think about life.

That evening as the emperor was going towards his palace, he noticed a Sadhu lying in the centre of his garden. He could not believe his eyes. A strange Sadhu, in ragged clothes, right in the middle of the palace garden? The guards would have to be punished for this, thought the emperor furiously as he walked over to that Sadhu and prodded him with the tip of his embroidered slipper.

"Here, fellow!" he cried. "What are you doing here? Get up and go away at once!"

That Sadhu opened his eyes. Then he sat up slowly and said in a sleepy voice. "Is this your garden?"

"Yes!" cried the Emperor. "This garden those rose bushes, the fountain beyond that, the courtyard, the palace, this fort, this empire, it all belongs to me!"
Slowly that Sadhu stood up. "And the river? And the city? And this country?".
"Yes, yes, it's all mine", said the emperor. "Now get out!"

"Ah", said the Sadhu. "And before you, who did the garden and fort and city belong to then?"

"My father, of course", said the emperor. In spite of his irritation, he was beginning to get interested in the Sadhu's questions. He loved philosophical discussions and he could tell, from his manner of speaking, that the Sadhu was a learned man.

"And who was here before him?" the Sadhu asked quietly.

"His father, my father's father, as you know."

"Ah", said the Sadhu. So this garden, those rose bushes, the palace and the fort all this has only belonged to you for your lifetime. Before that they belonged to your father, am I right? And after yours time they will belong to your son, and then to his son?

"Yes", said the Emperor Akbar wonderingly.

"So each one stays here for a time and then goes on his

ways?"

"Yes."

"Like a dharmashala (inn)?" the Sadhu asked. "No one owns a dharmashala. Or the shade of a tree on the side of a road. We stop and rest for a while and then go on. And someone has always been there before us and someone will always come after we have gone. Is that not so?"

"It is", Emperor Akbar quietly.

"So your garden, your palace, your fort, your empire, these are only places you will stay in for a time, for the span of your lifetime. When you die, they will no longer belong to you. You will go, leaving them in the possession of someone else, just as your father did and his father before him."

Emperor Akbar nodded. "The whole world is a dharmashala", he said slowly, thinking very hard. "In which we mortals rest awhile. That's what you are telling me, isn't it? Nothing on this earth can ever belong to a single person, because each person is only passing through the earth and must die one day?"

The Sadhu nodded earnestly. Then, bowing to the ground, he removed his white beard and saffron turban and his voice changed. "Your majesty, forgive me!" he said, in his normal voice. "It was my way of asking you to think about..."

"Birbal, oh, Birbal!" the emperor exclaimed. "You are wiser than any philosopher. Come, come at once to the royal chamber and let us discuss this further. Even emperors are but wayfarers on the path of life, it is clear!"

Birbal Betrays Himself

Birbal was missing. He and the emperor had a quarrel and Birbal had stormed out of the palace vowing never to return. Now Akbar missed him and wanted him back but no one knew where he was. Then the emperor had a brainwave. He offered a reward of 100 gold coins to any man who could come to the palace observing the following condition. The man had to walk in the sun without an umbrella but he had to be in the shade at the same time.

"Impossible," said the people. Then a villager came carrying a string cot over his head and claimed the prize. "I've walked in the sun but at the same time I was in the shade of the strings of the cot," he said.

It was a brilliant solution. On interrogation the villager confessed that the idea had been suggested to him by a man living with him. "It could only be Birbal!" said the emperor, delighted.

Sure enough it was Birbal and he and the emperor had a joyous reunion.

Birbal Denies Rumour

One day a man stopped Birbal in the street and began narrating his woes to him. "I've walked twenty miles to see you", he told Birbal finally, "and all along the way people kept saying you were the most generous man in the country."

Birbal knew the man was going to ask him for money.

"Are you going back the same way?" he asked.

"Yes," said the man.

"Will you do me a favour?"

"Certainly," said the man. "What do you want me to do?"

"Please deny the rumour of my generosity," said Birbal, walking away.

Birbal Identifies Thief.

One fine morning, a minister from Emperor Akbar's court had gathered in the assembly hall. He informed the Emperor that all his valuables had been stolen by a thief the previous night. Akbar was shocked to hear this because the place where that minister lived was the safest place in the kingdom.

He invited Birbal to solve the mystery. Akbar said "It is definitely not possible for an outsider to enter into the minister's house and steal the valuables. This blunder is definitely committed only by another minister of that court". Saying so, he arranged for a donkey to be tied to a pillar. He ordered all the courtiers to lift the donkey's tail and say "I have not stolen."

Birbal added "Only then we can judge the culprit." After everyone had finished, he asked the courtiers to show their palm to him. All the courtiers except Amir Khan had a black patch of paint on their palm.

Birbal had actually painted the donkey's tail with a black coat of paint. In the fright, the guilty minister did not touch the donkey's tail at all.

Thus Birbal once again proved his astuteness and was rewarded by the king with 100 gold coins.

Birbal returns home

Birbal was in Persia at the invitation of the king of that country. Parties were given in his honour and rich presents were heaped on him. On the eve of his departure for home, a nobleman asked him how he would compare the king of Persia to his own king.

"Your king is a full moon," said Birbal. "Whereas mine could be likened to the quarter moon."

The Persians were very happy. But when Birbal got home

he found that Emperor Akbar was furious with him. "How could you belittle your own king!" demanded Akbar. "You are a traitor!"

"No Majesty," said Birbal. "I did not belittle you. The full moon diminishes and disappears whereas the quarter moon grows from strength to strength. What I, in fact, proclaimed to the world is that your power is growing from day to day whereas that of the king of Persia is about to go into decline."

Akbar grunted in approval and welcomed Birbal back with a warm embrace.

Birbal Shortens the Road

The Emperor Akbar was travelling to a distant place along with some of his courtiers. It was a hot day and the emperor was tiring of the journey.

"Can't anybody shorten this road for me?" he asked, querulously. "I can," said Birbal. The other courtiers looked at one another, perplexed. All of them knew there was no other path through the hilly terrain. The road they were travelling on was the only one that could take them to their destination.

"You can shorten the road?" said the emperor. "Well, do it."

"I will," said Birbal. "Listen first to this story I have to tell."

And riding beside the emperor's palanquin, he launched upon a long and intriguing tale that held Akbar and all those listening, spellbound. Before they knew it, they had reached the end of their journey.

"We've reached?" exclaimed Akbar. "So soon!"

"Well," grinned Birbal, "you did say you wanted the road to be shortened."

Birbal's sweet reply

One day the Emperor Akbar shocked his courtiers with a strange question.

"If somebody pulled my moustache what sort of punishment should be given to him?" he asked.

"He should be flogged!" said one courtier.

"He should be hanged!" said another.

"He should be beheaded!" said a third.

"And what about you, Birbal?" asked the emperor. "What do you think would be the right thing to do if somebody pulled my whiskers?"

"He should be given sweets," said Birbal.

"Sweets?" gasped the other couriers.

"Yes", said Birbal. "Sweets, because the only one who would dare pull His Majesty's moustache is his grandson."

So pleased was the emperor with the answer that he pulled off his ring and gave it to Birbal as a reward.

Birbal the Servant

One day Akbar and Birbal were riding through the countryside and they happened to pass by a cabbage patch.

"Cabbages are such delightful vegetables!" said Akbar. "I just love cabbage."

"The cabbage is king of vegetables!" said Birbal.

A few weeks later they were riding past the cabbage patch again.

This time however, the emperor made a face when he saw the vegetables. "I used to love cabbage but now I have no taste for it." said Akbar.

"The cabbage is a tasteless vegetable" agreed Birbal.

The emperor was astonished.

"But the last time you said it was the king of vegetables!" he said.

"I did," admitted Birbal. "But I am your servant Your Majesty, not the cabbage's."

Birbal Turns Tables

Emperor Akbar was narrating a dream.

The dream began with Akbar and Birbal walking towards each other on a moonless night.

It was so dark that they could not see each other and they collided and fell.

"Fortunately for me," said the Emperor. "I fell into a pool of payasam. But guess what Birbal fell into?"

"What, your Majesty?" asked the courtiers.

"A gutter!"

The court resounded with laughter. The emperor was thrilled that for once he had been able to score over Birbal.

But Birbal was at ease.

"Your Majesty," he said when the laughter had died down. "Strangely, I too had the same dream. But unlike you I slept on till the end. When you climbed out of that pool of delicious payasam and I, out of that stinking gutter we found that there was no water with which to clean ourselves and so guess what we did?"

"What?" asked the emperor, warily.

"We licked each other clean!"

The emperor became red with embarrassment and resolved never to try to get the better of Birbal again.

Cooking the Khichdi

It was winter. The ponds were all frozen.

At the court, Akbar asked Birbal, "Tell me Birbal! Will a man do anything for money?" Birbal replied, 'Yes'.

The emperor ordered him to prove it.

The next day Birbal came to the court along with a poor Brahmin who merely had a penny left with him. His family was starving.

Birbal told the king that the Brahmin was ready to do anything for the sake of money.

The king ordered the Brahmin to be inside the frozen pond all through the night without any attire if he needed money.

The poor Brahmin had no choice. The whole night he was inside the pond, shivering. He returned to the durbar the next day to receive his reward.

The king asked "Tell me Oh poor Brahmin! How could you withstand the extreme temperature all through the night?". The innocent Brahmin replied "I could see a faintly glowing light a mile away and I withstood with that ray of light."

Akbar refused to pay the Brahmin his reward saying that he had got warmth from the light and withstood the cold and that was cheating. The poor Brahmin could not argue with him and so returned disappointed and bare-handed. Birbal tried to explain to the king but the king was in no mood to listen to him.

Thereafter, Birbal stopped coming to the durbar and sent a messenger to the king saying that he would come to the court only after cooking his khichdi. As Birbal did not turn up even after 5 days, the king himself went to Birbal's house to see what he was doing. Birbal had lit the fire and kept the pot of uncooked khichdi one meter away from it.

Akbar questioned him "How will the khichdi get cooked with the fire one meter away? What is wrong with you Birbal?"

Birbal, cooking the khichdi, replied "Oh my great King of Hindustan! When it was possible for a person to receive warmth from a light that was a kilometer away, then it is possible for this khichdi, which is just a meter away from the source of heat, to get cooked."

Akbar understood his mistake. He called the poor Brahmin and rewarded him 200 gold coins.

Half the reward

Mahesh Das was a citizen in the kingdom of Akbar. He was an intelligent young man. Once when Akbar went hunting in the jungle, he lost his way. Mahesh Das who lived in the outer edge helped the king reach the palace. The emperor rewarded him with his ring.

The Emperor also promised to give him a responsible posting at his court. After a few days Mahesh Das went to the court. The guard did not allow him to enter. Mahesh Das showed the guard the ring which the king had given him. Now the guard thought that the young man was sure to get more rewards by the king. The greedy guard agreed to allow him inside the court on one condition. It was that Mahesh Das had to pay him half the reward he would get from the Emperor. Mahesh Das accepted the condition.

He then entered the court and showed the ring to the King. The King who recognized Mahesh asked him "Oh young man! What do you expect as a reward from the King of Hindustan?" "Majesty! I expect 50 lashes from you as a reward." replied Mahesh Das.

The courtiers were stunned. They thought that he was mad. Akbar pondered over his request and asked him the reason. Mahesh Das said he would tell him the reason after receiving his reward. Then the king's men whipped him as per his wish. After the 25th lash Mahesh Das requested the King to call the guard who was at the gate.

The guard appeared before the King. He was happy at the thought that he was called to be rewarded. But to his surprise, Mahesh Das told the King ,"This greedy guard let me inside on condition that I pay him half the reward I receive from you. I wanted to teach him a lesson. Please give the remaining 25 lashes to this guard so that I can keep my promise to him."

The King then ordered that the guard be given 25 lashes. The King was very happy with Mahesh Das. He called him Raja Birbal and made him his minister.

Identify the guest

Birbal had been invited to lunch by a rich man. Birbal went to the man's house and found him in a hall full of people.

His host greeted him cordially. "I did not know there would be so many guests," said Birbal who hated large gatherings. "They are not guests," said the man. "They are my workforce, all except one man. He is the only other guest here beside you."

Then a sneaky look came on the man's face. "Can you tell me which of them the guest is?" he asked.

"Maybe I could," said Birbal. "Talk to them as I observe them. Tell them a joke or something."

The man told a joke that Birbal thought was perhaps the worst he had heard in a long time. When he finished everyone laughed wildly.

"Well," said the rich man. "I've told my joke. Now tell me who my other guest is."

Birbal pointed out the man to him.

"How did you know?" asked his host, amazed.

"workers tend to laugh at any joke told by their employers," explained Birbal. "When I saw that this man was the only one not laughing at your joke, and in fact, looked positively bored, I at once knew he was your other guest."

Just One Question

One Day a scholar came to the court of Emperor Akbar and challenged Birbal to answer his questions and thus prove that he was as clever as people said he was.

He asked Birbal: "Would you prefer to answer a hundred easy questions or just a single difficult one?"

Both the emperor and Birbal had had a difficult day and were impatient to leave.

"Ask me one difficult question," sad Birbal.

"Well, then, tell me," said the man, "which came first into the world, the chicken or the egg?"

"The chicken," replied Birbal.

"How do you know?" asked the scholar, a note of achievement in his voice.

"We had agreed you would ask only one question and you have already asked it" said Birbal and he and the emperor walked away leaving the scholar gaping.

Limping Horse

A nobleman's prized racehorse began to limp for no apparent reason.

Veterinarians who were called found nothing wrong with

the leg - no fracture, no sprain and no soreness - and they were baffled.

The nobleman finally consulted a sage, a man known for his wisdom.

"Has anything changed for the horse in the last few months?" he asked.

"I changed his trainer a few weeks ago," said the nobleman.

"Does the horse get on well with his new trainer?"

"Very well! In fact, he's devoted to him."

"Does the trainer limp?"

"Uh… yes, he does."

"The reason for the horse's limp is clear," said the sage. "He's imitating his handler. We all tend to imitate those whom we admire. The company we keep has a great influence on us."

The nobleman put the horse in the charge of another trainer and the horse soon stopped limping.

List of blinds

Once King Akbar questioned Birbal if he knows the number of blind citizens of their kingdom.

Birbal had requested Akbar to give him a week's time to find out.

The next day Birbal was found to be mending shoes in the town market. People were astonished to see Birbal doing such work. Many of them started to question "Birbal!! What are you doing?"

Once when he was asked this question by someone he started writing something. It continued for a week when on the 7th day King Akbar himself asked Birbal the same question.

Giving him no answer, Birbal reported at the court the next day and handed over a note to King Akbar. Akbar read the note when he found that it was the big list of people who were blind.

Emperor Akbar was stunned when he found his own name in the list. Angered by this, Akbar asked Birbal the reason for writing his name in the list.

Birbal said "O! My majesty! Like all other people you also saw me mending the slippers but you still asked me what I was doing. Therefore I had to include your name too."

Akbar started laughing at this and everyone enjoyed Birbal's sense of humour.

Noble Beggar

Emperor Akbar asked Birbal if it was possible for a man to be the lowest and the noblest at the same time.

"It is possible," said Birbal.

"Then bring me such a person," said the emperor.

Birbal went out and returned with a beggar.

"He is the lowest among your subjects," he said, presenting him to Akbar.

"That might be true," said Akbar. "But I don't see how he can be the noblest."

"He has been given the honour of an audience with the emperor," said Birbal. "That makes him the noblest among beggars."

Painting by Birbal

Once Akbar told Birbal, "Birbal, make me a painting. Use imagination in it." To which the reply was "but sir, I am a minister, how can I possibly paint?" The king was angry and said "If I don't get a good painting by one week then you shall be hanged!"

The clever Birbal had an idea. After one week, he went to the court and with him he carried a covered frame.

Akbar was happy to see that Birbal had obeyed him, until he opened the cover. The courtiers rushed to see what was wrong. What they saw made them feel very happy. At last, they would not see Birbal in court! The painting was nothing but ground and sky. There were a few specs of green on the ground.

The Emperor, angrily, told Birbal 'what is this?' To which the reply was "a cow eating grass".

Akbar said "where is the cow and grass?" and Birbal told "I used my imagination. The cow ate the grass and returned to its shed!"

Question for Question

One day Akbar said to Birbal: "Can you tell me how many bangles your wife wears?" Birbal said he could not.

"You cannot?" exclaimed Akbar. "You see her hands every day while she serves you food. Yet you do not know how many bangles she has on her hands? How is that?"

"Let us go down to the garden, Your Majesty," said Birbal, "and I'll tell you."

They went down the small staircase that led to the garden. Then Birbal turned to the emperor: "Your Majesty," he said, "You go up and down this staircase every day. Can you tell me how many steps there are in the staircase?"

The emperor grinned and quickly changed the subject.

The Blind Saint

There lived a saint in an ashram in the kingdom of Emperor Akbar.

He was believed to foretelling the future correctly. Once he had a visitor who had come to treat their niece. The child's parents were killed in front of the girl's eyes. Once she saw the saint, she started to scream loudly saying that that saint was the culprit. Angered by the girl's words, the saint demanded the couple to get away with their child. The whole day the girl cried which made the couple to realize that the girl was not lying.

Therefore, they decided to seek the help of Birbal. Birbal consoled them and asked them to wait at the Emperor's assembly. Birbal had invited the saint to Akbar's court too. Then in front of all the ministers he drew a sword and neared the saint to kill him. The saint in panic immediately drew another sword and began to fight. Thus by this act of the saint it was proved that he wasn't blind.

Therefore, Akbar demanded to hang the culprit and

rewarded the girl for her bravery for telling the truth even at the critical situation.

The loyal gardener

One day the Emperor Akbar stumbled on a rock in his garden. He was in a foul mood that day and the accident made him so angry that he ordered the gardener's arrest and execution. The next day when the gardener was asked what his last wish was before he was hanged, he requested an audience with the emperor.

This wish was granted, but when the man neared the throne he loudly cleared his throat and spat at the emperor's feet. The emperor was taken aback and demanded to know why he had done such a thing. The gardener had acted on Birbal's advice and now Birbal stepped forward in the man's justification.

"Your Majesty," he said, "there could be no person more loyal to you than this unfortunate man. Fearing that people would say you hanged him for a trifle, he has gone out of his way to give you a genuine reason for hanging him."

The emperor, realizing that he had been about to do a great injustice, set the man free.

The Sharpest Shield and Sword

A man who made spears and shields once came to Akbar's court.

"Your Majesty, nobody can make shields and spears to equal mine," he said. "My shields are so strong that nothing can pierce them and my spears are so sharp that there's nothing they cannot pierce."

"I can prove you wrong on one count certainly," said Birbal suddenly.

"Not possible!" declared the man.

"Hold up one of your shields and I will pierce it with one of your spears," said Birbal with a grin.

The True King

The King of Iran had heard that Birbal was one of the wisest men in the East and wishing for meeting him sent him an invitation to visit his country.

In due course, Birbal arrived in Iran.

When he entered the palace he was stunned to find not

one but six kings seated there.

All looked alike. All were dressed in kingly robes. Who was the real king?

The very next moment he got his answer. Confidently, he approached the king and bowed to him.

"But how did you identify me?" the king asked, puzzled.

Birbal smiled and explained: "The false kings were all looking at you, while you yourself looked straight ahead. Even in regal robes, the common people will always look to their king for support."

Delighted, the king embraced Birbal and showered him with gifts.

The Well Dispute

Once there was a complaint at King Akbar's court. There were two neighbors who shared their garden. In that garden, there was a well that was possessed by Ibrahim.

His neighbour, who was a farmer wanted to buy the well for irrigation purpose. Therefore they signed an agreement between them, after which the farmer owned the well.

Even after selling the well to the farmer, Ibrahim continued to fetch water from the well. Angered by this, the farmer had come to get justice from King Akbar.

King Akbar asked Ibrahim the reason for fetching water from the well even after selling it to the farmer.

Ibrahim replied that he had sold only the well to the farmer but not the water inside it.

King Akbar wanted Birbal who was present in the court listening to the problem to solve the dispute.

Birbal came forward and gave a solution. He said " Ibrahim, You say that you have sold only the well to the farmer. And you claim that the water is yours. Then how come you can keep your water inside another person's well without paying rent?"

Ibrahim's trickery was countered thus in a tricky way. The farmer got justice and Birbal was fairly rewarded.

Around the campfire

Once while travelling, Raman found himself in the company of a group of soldiers. They were all veterans of war and soon they got to talking about their experiences on the battlefield. One old soldier told of the time he had single-handedly slain seven enemy soldiers.

Another gave a detailed description of the manner in which he had held an entire enemy battalion at bay. When they had finished they looked condescendingly at Raman.

"I don't suppose you have any adventure worth telling," said one of the grizzled warriors.

"Oh, but I have," said Rama

"You have?!" said the soldiers.

"Yes," said Rama. "Once while travelling I chanced upon a large tent. I entered and there, lying on a mat was the largest man I had ever seen. I recognized him at once as a dreaded dacoit who had been terrorizing that part of the country for years!"

"What did you do?" asked the soldiers, their interest now fully aroused.

"I cut off his toe and ran for dear life," said Rama.

"His toe?" said a soldier. "Why toe? You should have cut off his head while you had the chance!"

"Somebody had already done that," said Rama, grinning.

Meera

It was a cold chilly winter morning. Meera was on her way to work when she noticed a homeless man sitting outside a coffee shop waiting, that someone will offer him a hot brew. She looked at her watch and thought I need to be at work in the next 5 minutes and I will help this homeless man on another occasion. She wanted to do the deed but she kept reasoning that someone will sure help him, but it's just not her this time.

Meera walked past the man without meeting his gaze but heard his feeble voice saying can someone be generous and feed him? The next thing she heard was her mobile ring and "office calling" flashing on her screen. She answered only to know that her boss was at his desk already, waiting for her to discuss the agenda for the meeting ahead. She hurried to her workplace and got lost in her pile of work; although the old homeless man did not once leave her mind. She was restless and could not deliver the expected in her meeting.

The platters of food, flasks of hot coffee and fresh fruit made her stomach churn; knowing that someone somewhere was hungry. After the meeting, her boss asked her to prepare herself better for the next one post lunch for this was her last chance to impress and bag the long awaited promotion she wanted. She knew she couldn't afford to go wrong this time.

The old man had nothing to do with her work or her meeting, yet she was not at peace somehow. She promised to put his thought behind and concentrate on her work. Meera went back to her desk and sat calm, thinking how she can get it right for her next meeting. She had to deliver by hook or by crook. But thoughts wouldn't flow. She only kept thinking about the hungry soul hoping he would have been fed by now. And her thoughts drifted back to the days when she was new to this city. She had come here alone to live her dreams of making it big in a big city and had limited resources. Even she, then, had combined her lunch and dinner and had only one meal a day. A tear escaped her watery eyes. She knew the answer to her restlessness.

With all eagerness, Meera ran to her boss and promised him that she will be back from lunch and give her best presentation. Grabbing her bag, she ran to the coffee shop only to find the old homeless man not in his place. She could feel her blood flush to her eyes and started looking around. There he was, almost reaching the end of the road and about to vanish in the busy streets.

She ran to him calling out saying "excuse me, excuse me sir.". He turned around least expecting that the call was for him. She stopped next to him, trying to catch her breath. He looked puzzled and asked if it was him that she was calling for. She smiled and said yes. She asked him if he can join her for lunch, that she would be happy to have a meal with him. He couldn't believe her at first and then with tears in his eyes, agreed saying he had not eaten since 2days and that not all people around are as good as she was. Meera felt a pang of guilt and sobbed quietly. She took him to the nearby coffee shop, they both had a sandwich and a coffee, and she got him some more food for later. With folded hands, the gentleman blessed her saying that hunger is hard to bare but it's good humans like her that make the delay worth while. Meera could not take the kind words of the old man and started crying. She vowed that no matter what, she will always spare time and help people like this old man who only had kind words and blessings for her.

With content in her heart, Meera returned to her office only to give her best presentation. She was appreciated by all, and specially for the big smile on her face. Only she knew the reason for it!

The following day Meera was glad to see that the restaurant that she had had lunch the previous day, was now offering free meals to homeless people.

Moral of the story: *Always help the needy when you can, don't wait for the right time. Spread goodness, do your part and the world will follow.*

Mayonnaise and Coffee Experiemnt

A professor stood before his philosophy class and had some items in front of him. When the class began, wordlessly, he picked up a very large and empty mayonnaise Jar and proceeded to fill it with golf balls.

He then asked the students if the Jar was full. They agreed that it was. So the professor then picked up a box of pebbles and poured them into the Jar. He shook the Jar lightly. The pebbles rolled into the open areas between the golf balls. He then asked the students again if the Jar was full. They agreed it was.
The professor next picked up a box of sand and poured it into the Jar. Of course, the sand filled up everything else. He asked once more if the Jar was full. The students responded unanimous "yes."

The professor then produced two cups of Coffee from under the table and poured the entire contents into the Jar, effectively filling the empty space between the sand. The students laughed.

"Now," said the professor, as the laughter subsided, "I want you to recognize that this Jar represents your life. The golf balls are the important things, your God, family, your children, your health, your friends, and your favourite passions things that if everything else was lost and only they remained, your life would still be full." The pebbles are the other things that matter like your job, your house, and your car. The sand is everything else the small stuff.

"If you put the sand into the Jar first," he continued, "there is no room for the pebbles or the golf balls." The same goes for life. If you spend all your time and energy on the small stuff, you will never have room for the things that are important. Pay attention to the things that are critical to your happiness. Play with your children. Take care of the golf balls first, the things that really matter. Set your priorities. The rest is just sand.

One of the students raised her hand and inquired what the Coffee represented. The professor smiled. "I'm glad you asked. It just goes to show you that no matter how full your life may seem, there's always room for a couple of cups of Coffee with a friend."

Ca, Ca, and Ca

There lived a tiny girl and she had tiny golden curls. She had few friends. A family of peafowls was her playmates. She named them Neeli, Chabilli, Ca, Ca, and Ca. Neeli , the father peafowl had a train of the blue coloured long tail which he spread like a rainbow when he danced with the tiny Tia.

Chabili, the pea hen, had no feather at all. Tia felt bad for her. But she knew if Chabili had long feathers like the daddy peacock how would she run around the naughty Ca, Ca, and Ca. They were as naughty as the boy next window. He would always throw the chocolate wrappers and the orange peels from the window. It made Tia furious. Her mother would always ask her to use a dustbin and not litter around. Ca, Ca, and Ca always picked the wrappers assuming as food but got disappointed.

Ca, Ca, and Ca, were Neeli and Chabilli's three kids. They appeared identical and added to the little girl's plight. They rambled in a shrill voice CAA, CAA, CAA and thus their name. Pea fowls are common in Jaipur. Their habitat is stolen by the jungle concrete and so they are lost among humans. Human – not all to be trusted. However, with Tia it was different. She was a friend to the pigeons, sparrows and doves. They would dance with the tipy tapy rains, to the whisper of the wind, at the sizzle of the Ashoka leaves and the shades of the clouds. But most of the time, it was the traffic. She lived by the road in an apartment with her parents.

Tia tried growing taller and bigger by standing on her toes to reach the peacock's feathers when it would merrily dance at the thunderous shake of the clouds. She was just 6 and it won't work. She was tiny. She did not like going to school. She brought bread for the tiffin that her mother baked. The school disapproved. She once packed a kitten in her bag which jumped off during the attendance.

Her father had a book store. She heard her father complaining that nobody read books these days. She loved the smell of the books from their store. It reminded her of the whistle of the train when she travelled with her mom in summers. They don't go now. The alphabets and the characters would float around her when her father read aloud those stories to her. She could make games from everything around her. The world was her home for games .She would tell those stories to her bird brigade while she shared Choco-chip cookies to them. Her mother baked cookies, muffins, and brownies for her.

Days passed by and brought happier days. From solitude to school, she grew up. With her profound memories of moments in solitude, she created a world of her own. Tia converted the book store to a library cum bakeshop. Many pea fowls now came there to play with Tia and all the kids who came to read, also bake their favourite walnut brownie.

The Legendary Ball of Rapid Fire

Once upon a time there lived two aliens in planet Xandar. They are Robert Clove and Dorajeera. They are best friends. They live a rich and happy life.

Dorajeera has a good habit of reading newspaper daily. After reading the newspaper dated 19-5-3911 he was under a shock as the newspaper said that there was a ball named the legendary ball of rapid fire which will fulfil all the wishes of its owner. So Dorajeera immediately called Robert clove and invited him to his house. Then Robert clove immediately rushed to Dorajeera's house. Dorajeera told the shocking news about the legendary ball of rapid fire to him, he too was shocked. And soon they decided to go, find and get it.

After searching for about a month when they almost left their hopes, they found the entrance to the place where the ball resides. But after getting there they found that to achieve the ball they must go through a series of rapid-fire questions test to prove the ball's guardian that they are worthy to own the ball. They had tough time clearing all questions but they answered all questions correctly. The guardian then allowed them to take the ball with them.

So, after taking the ball they went back to their home. So,

they at last achieved the ball, they were overjoyed and asked all the wishes they had and they were granted by the legendary ball of rapid fire.

Many days passed and nobody in Xandar could defeat the strength and the capability of the alien friends. But with great power comes great responsibility, they always handled the responsibility by not showing partiality to only some people they used the ball for all good causes. But, over the time the aliens became so greedy for more power that they came to a point, where they asked the legendary ball of rapid fire to create a legendary power which is more powerful than the ball itself. Then the ball blasted and all the people died and the entire civilization got erased from history.

Nothing could destroy them but, the aliens' own greed erased them along with their whole civilization. Always be happy with what u have and don't be greedy for what u don't have as it may lead you to your own downfall.

Crux of the Mahabharata Story and lessons learnt

The narrative begins with Hastinapur's King Shantanu of the Kuru dynasty marrying river Goddess Ganga. Bhishma, one of the prominent characters in Mahabharata, was their son. Ganga left them to carry out her godly duties, and Shantanu married Satyavati and had two sons with her. Vichitravirya, one of the sons, became the king after him. He fathered three sons, Dhritarashtra, Pandu and Vidur. Dhritarashtra being blind, Pandu became the king supported by Bhishma.

Dhritarashtra married Gandhari and had a hundred sons, the Kauravas. Pandu married Kunti and Madri, and with the blessings of different gods, the five Pandavas were born. Unknown to everyone, Kunti was already an unwed mother to her oldest son, Karna.

Having brought prosperity to his kingdom, Pandu decided to leave to the forest, entrusting the kingdom to the care of Dhritarashtra. After Pandu and Madri's death, Kunti came back to Hastinapur with the five boys. The cousins, Kauravas, and Pandavas never got along. There were failed attempts by the Kauravas to kill them. And after one such conspiracy, the Pandavas with their mother went into hiding. In this period, Arjun married Draupadi, and they all went back to Hastinapur. But they were exiled to the forest for thirteen years when in a game of dice, Yudhishthir lost everything to the Kauravas.

On their return, Duryodhana refused to give back the territory, and the stage was set for the greatest battle despite Lord Krishna's attempts to bring peace. The war went on for eighteen days and ended with the defeat of the Kauravas. Yudhishthir was crowned the King.

Moral Lessons from Mahabharata

- Be focused, and you will always succeed.
- A teacher can guide you and inspire you, but practice will make you perfect.
- Keep good company. Bad friends will bring about your downfall.
- Respect women. The disrespect shown to women will bring disasters upon you.
- Don't indulge in vices like gambling. You will end up losing everything.
- Don't give up easily. Fight for what is rightfully yours. Truth always wins in the end.
- Don't apply half-learned knowledge to your actions. It will only lead to failure.
- Don't support the wrong acts of your close friends and relatives. It will bring trouble upon you as well.
- Do not seek revenge. Vengeance spells the end for the seeker and the sought both.

- War is never good. Matters can be resolved with dialogue.

Like any great epic, Mahabharata too is the story of victory of good against evil. The word 'Mahabharata' has become synonymous with any great conflict in day to day life also. But its moral lessons will be synonymous with the right and honest way of life.

Tales from Ramayana

The Story of a Squirrel

After the abduction of Sita, Lord Rama along with this army of monkey and bears starts making a bridge over the sea that would connect them to Lanka. Lord Rama was triumphant to see the passion, dedication and energy level of his army towards the construction of the bridge. A little squirrel was picking up a pebble in her mouth and putting it near the boulders. She did it repeatedly and effortlessly.

Just then, a monkey noticed her and started making fun of her. He told her to stay away lest a boulder crush her. Hearing this, everyone started making fun of her. The squirrel was in tears. Lord Rama was noticing all this from a distance.

Upset, the squirrel went to Lord Rama and complained about everyone to him. Lord Rama then demonstrated to the Army how the pebble thrown by the squirrel has worked as the connector between the two boulders. Even her contribution is as valuable as the other members of the army.

Acknowledging the squirrel's effort, Lord Rama stroked

the squirrel's back. The stroking left the marks of his finger on the body of the squirrel. Since then, the squirrels have carried white stripes on their body.

The Story Behind Ravana's 10 Heads

Ravana was a devout follower of Lord Shiva. After attaining the education, Ravana underwent an intense penance to please Lord Shiva. To appease Lord Shiva, Ravana even chopped off his head. Each time he chopped off his head, it grew back, thereby enabling him to continue his penance. This austerity of Ravana pleased Shiva, and he granted him ten heads. And thus, he became one of the most powerful beings on the earth. The ten heads of Ravana indicate the four Vegas and six shashtras that Ravana mastered. It can be the best Ramayana stories for kids to know about the great epic Ramayana.

Laxman Defeating Sleep for 14 Years

Urmila, Laxman's wife, was ready to accompany him when he was leaving for the exile, but Laxman forced her to stay home. Laxman wanted to protect Ram and Sita from all the dangers, defeating sleep. So he approached Nindra, the Goddess of Sleep and asked her to look over him for the next 14 years. Nindra commanded that someone had to sleep on behalf of him to create a balance. So Laxman asked her to consider Urmila for this. Nindra went to the palace of Ayodhya and asked Urmila if she would like to take up Laxman's sleep, to which she gladly agreed.

Urmila slept for 14 years, until the day of Ram's coronation. If Urmila had not helped, Laxman would have never been able to slay Megnath, the one who was granted a boon that only Gudakesh could kill him.

Surpanakha, the Stimulus of the Battle of Lanka

Most accounts of Ramayana suggest that Surpanakha, Ravana's sister had no interest in Rama. But Valmiki's Ramayana accounts that Surpanakha approached Rama, but he rejected her for Sita. Soorpnakha then proposed to Laxman, but even he rejected her. Angered by the rejection, Surpanakha tried to hurt Sita. Fearing Sita's life, Rama told Laxman to chop off her ears and nose. To seek revenge, Surpanakha induced Ravana to kidnap Sita, which triggered the battle.

But other accounts suggest that Surpanakha enticed Ravana to kidnap Sita to avenge her husband's death. Surpanakha was first married to Dushtabuddhi Rakasha, who enjoyed great favors from Ravana, But his greed for more enraged Ravana and he had him killed. Distraught by the death of Dushtabuddhi Rakasha, Surpnakha realized that only Rama could kill Ravana. So, when Laxman chopped off her nose, she provoked Ravana to kidnap Sita as an act of revenge.

Hanuman receives Sita's Pearl Necklace

After coming back victorious from the battle, Rama was rewarding everyone who helped him in the battle. When he asked Hanuman what he wanted as a gift, Hanuman refused to take anything. Watching this exchange, Sita gave Hanuman her pearl necklace. Hanuman accepted the gift, and he started breaking each pearl with his teeth. Astonished, Sita asked Hanuman why he was breaking the pearls, and he replied that he was looking for Rama in the pearls, but he can't find him. The ministers of the court started mocking Hanuman for his devotion, and one of them asked Hanuman if his body also has Rama in it. In response, Hanuman tore his chest apart with his hands and residing in his heart was the image of Rama and Sita. Everyone was shocked by his devotion and congratulated him.

The illusion of reflection

Once there was a king who had presented his daughter, the princess, with a beautiful diamond necklace. The necklace was stolen and his people in the kingdom searched everywhere but could not find it. Some said a bird might have stolen it. The king then asked them all to search for it and put a reward for 5,000 for anyone who found it.

One day a clerk was walking home along a river next to an industrial area. This river was completely polluted, filthy and smelly. As he was walking, the clerk saw a shimmering in the river and when he looked, he saw the diamond necklace. He decided to try and catch it so that he could get the 5,000 reward. He put his hand in the filthy, dirty river and grabbed at the necklace, but somehow missed it and didn't catch it. He took his hand out and looked again and the necklace was still there. He tried again, this time he walked in the river and dirtied his pants in the filthy river and put his whole arm in to catch the necklace. But strangely, he still missed the necklace! He came out and started walking away, feeling depressed.

Then again he saw the necklace, right there. This time he was determined to get it, no matter what. He decided to plunge into the river, although it was a disgusting thing to do as the river was polluted, and his whole body would become filthy. He plunged in, and searched everywhere for the necklace and yet he failed. This time he was really bewildered and came out feeling very depressed that he could not get the necklace that would get him Rs50,000.

Just then a saint who was walking by, saw him, and asked him what the matter was. The clerk didn't want to share the secret with the saint, thinking the saint might take the necklace for himself, so he refused to tell the saint anything. But the saint could see this man was troubled and being compassionate, again asked the clerk to tell him the problem and promised that he would not tell anyone about it. The clerk mustered some courage and decided to put some faith in the saint. He told the saint about the necklace and how he tried and tried to catch it, but kept failing.

The saint then told him that perhaps he should try looking upward, toward the branches of the tree, instead of in the filthy river. The clerk looked up and trues enough, the necklace was dangling on the branch of a tree. He had been trying to capture a mere reflection of the real necklace all this time.

The clever King

There was a country long time ago where the people would change a king every year. The person who would become the king had to agree to a contract that he would be sent to an island after his one year of being a king.

One king finished his term and it was time for him to go to the island and live there. The people dressed him up in expensive clothes and put him on an elephant and took him around the cities to say goodbye to all the people. This was the moment of sadness for all the kings who ruled for one year. After saying farewell, the people took the king with a boat to Remote Island and left him there.

On their way back, they discovered a ship that had sunk just recently. They saw a young man who survived by holding on to a floating piece of wood. As they needed a new king, they picked up the young man and took him to their country. They requested him to be a king for a year. First he refused but later he agreed to be a king. People told him about all the rules and regulations and that how he will be sent to an island after one year.

After three days of being a king, he asked the ministers if they could show him the island where all the other kings were sent. They agreed and took him to the island. The island was covered with thick Jungles and sounds of vicious animals were heard coming out of them. The king went little bit inside to check. Soon he discovered the dead bodies of all the past kings. He understood that as soon as they were left in the island, the animals came and killed them.

The king went back to the country and collected 100 strong workers. He took them to the island and instructed them to clean the Jungle, remove all the deadly animals & cut down all excess trees.

He would visit the island every month to see how the work was progressing. In the first month, all the animals were removed and many trees were cut down. In the second month, the whole island was cleaned out. The king then told the workers to plant gardens in various parts of the island. He also took with himself useful animals like chickens, ducks, birds, goats, cows etc. In the third month, he ordered the workers to build big houses and docking stations for ships. Over the months, the island turned into a beautiful place.

The young king would wear simple clothes and spend very little from his earnings as a king. He sent all the earnings to the island for storage. When nine months passed like this, the king called the ministers and told them: "I know that I have to go the island after one year, but I would like to go there right now." But the ministers didn't agree to this and said that he has to wait for another 3 months to complete the year.

3 months passed and now it was a full year. The people dressed up the young king and put him on an elephant to take him around the country to say goodbye to others. However, this king is unusually happy to leave the kingdom.

People asked him, "All the other kings would cry at this moment and why are you laughing?"

He replied, "Don't you know what the wise people say? They say that when you came to this world as a baby, you were crying and everyone was smiling. Live such a life that when you are dying, you will be smiling and everyone around you will be crying. I have lived that life. While all the other kings were lost into the luxuries of the kingdom, I always thought about the future and planned for it. I turned the deadly island into a beautiful abode for me where I can stay peacefully."

The moral lesson from this story is about how we should live our life. The life of this world is to prepare for the life hereafter. In this life, we shouldn't get lost into the deceiving and attractive things of this world and forget about what is to come in the afterlife. Rather, even if we are kings, we should live a simple life.

We are just Messengers

I was parked in front of the mall wiping off my car. I had just come from the car wash and was waiting for my wife to get out of work. Coming my way from across the parking lot was what society would consider a bum. From the looks of him, he had no car, no home, no clean clothes, and no money.

There are times when you feel generous but there are other times that you just don't want to be bothered. This was one of those "don't want to be bothered times."

"I hope he doesn't ask me for any money," I thought. He didn't. He came and sat on the curb in front of the bus stop but he didn't look like he could have enough money to even ride the bus. After a few minutes he spoke. "That's a very pretty car," he said.

He was ragged but he had an air of dignity around him. His scraggly blond beard keeps more than his face warm. I said, "Thanks," and continued wiping off my car. He sat there quietly as I worked. The expected plea for money never came.

As the silence between us widened something inside said, "Ask him if he needs any help." I was sure that he would

say "yes" but I held true to the inner voice.
"Do you need any help?" I asked.

He answered in three simple but profound words that I shall never forget. We often look for wisdom in great men and women. We expect it from those of higher learning and accomplishments.

I expected nothing but an outstretched grimy hand. He spoke the three words that shook me. "Don't we all?" he said.

I was feeling high and mighty, successful and important, above a bum in the street, until those three words hit me like a twelve gauge shotgun. Don't we all?
I needed help. Maybe not for bus fare or a place to sleep, but I needed help. I reached in my wallet and gave him not only enough for bus fare, but enough to get a warm meal and shelter for the day. Those three little words still ring true. No matter how much you have, no matter how much you have accomplished, you need help too. No matter how little you have, no matter how loaded you are with problems, even without money or a place to sleep, you can give help.

Even if it's just a compliment, you can give that. You never know when you may see someone that appears to have it all. They are waiting on you to give them what they don't have. A different perspective on life, a glimpse at something beautiful, a respite from daily chaos that only you through a torn world can see.
Maybe the man was just a homeless stranger wandering the

streets.

Maybe he was more than that. maybe he was sent by a power that is great and wise, to messenger to a soul too comfortable in themselves. Maybe God looked down, called an Angel, dressed him like a bum, and then said, "Go messenger to that man cleaning the car, that man needs help." Don't we all?

The Old student

Vikram was a skilled artist an artisan. With great expertise and interest, he made such a nice and beautiful inkpot that it could be presented to the king. He expected that, appreciating his artistic skill, the king would encourage him as far as possible. So, with countless hopes and thousand of desires, he presented that inkpot to the king. In the beginning the king was very impressed by his artistic skill but afterwards an unpleasant event occurred that caused an extraordinary change in Vikram' s life and way of thinking.

When the king was observing the skilled artistry of the beautiful inkpot and Vikram was lost in the world of thoughts, the people informed that a scholar-literary person or jury is about to enter the court. As soon as the scholar entered, the king got so much absorbed in welcoming and talking to him that he forgot Vikram and his skilled artistry. This incident caused an adverse and deep effect on the heart of Vikram.

He realized that now he would not receive the encouragement he had expected and all his desires and hopes are useless now. But Vikram's high spirited mind did not allow him to be in peace, so he started thinking as to what he should do. He decided to do what the others have done and go on the same way that the others have gone (until now). Therefore, he decided to search for his lost hopes in the world of knowledge, literature and books. Although for a wise man that has passed the days of his young age, it was not easy to study with young children and to start right from the initial stage. But he did not have a choice. After all whenever the fish is taken out of water, it is fresh.

Worse than that, in the beginning he did not find any sort of interest in himself regarding reading and writing. Perhaps spending a long time in artistic works and handicraft was the reason for stagnancy in his scientific and literary talent. But neither his advanced age nor lack of capability, none of these could change his decision. With great enthusiasm and zeal for attaining knowledge, he strictly got busy with his studies, until another incident occurred:

The teacher who was teaching him, taught him this lesson: "The teacher believes that the skin of a dog becomes clean after tanning." Vikram repeated this sentence a lot of times so that at the time of examination he should be able to succeed. But when he was asked to answer this question, he said: "The dog believes that the skin of a teacher becomes clean after tanning."

The audience upon hearing this answer started laughing. It was clear for everybody that this old man is absolutely incapable of reading and writing. After this incident Vikram not only left the school, but he left the town and went towards the Jungle. By chance, he reached the foot of a mountain, where he saw that the water is falling drop by drop from the top and due to the continuous falling of water, a hole had been formed in that hard stone. He reflected for sometime, a good idea crossed his mind like lightning. And he said: "Maybe my heart is not ready to accept (knowledge) but it is not harder than this stone. It is impossible that continuous studying and hard work would be ineffective."

Therefore, he came back and with hard work, he got busy in the attainment of knowledge. As a result he was reckoned as one of the popular scholars of his time.

You never be too old to learn something new.